WORKING OUT

Karate

Jeff Savage

Crestwood House
Parsippany, New Jersey

Designer: Deborah Fillion
Photo credits
    Cover: Jeff Savage
    Jeff Savage: pp. 1, 4, 7, 15, 18, 30, 32, 33, 34, 35 (both), 37, 38, 40, 43
    Steven Silz: pp. 11, 24 (both), 26
    TriStar Pictures: p. 21

Published by Crestwood House, an imprint of Silver Burdett Press.
A Simon & Schuster Company
299 Jefferson Road, Parsippany, NJ 07054

First Edition

Printed in the United States of America

10 9 8 7 6 5 4 3 2 1

Library of Congress Cataloging-in-Publication Data
Savage, Jeff, 1961–
    Karate / by Jeff Savage.—1st ed.
        p. cm.— (Working Out)
    Includes index.
    ISBN 0-89686-854-0   Pbk 0-382-24946-1
    1. Karate—Juvenile literature. I. Title. II. Series.
GV1114.3.S29 1995
796.8'153—dc20   93-27206

Summary: A beginner's guide to karate. Includes history, basic techniques, an
overview of other martial arts, and a glossary of terms.

10729

CONTENTS

Black belt Tom Muzila shares his expertise with beginners.

CHAPTER 1

Making a Choice

I t was a warm summer night in Los Angeles, and the young karate students inside the Paramount **dojo** (club) had just finished an intense practice. Without speaking a word, the students gathered on the hardwood floor around their instructor, who was wearing a black belt wrapped around a white **gi** (uniform). The instructor's name was Tom Muzila, and he was ranked as a fifth-degree black belt. The young students knew that Muzila's expertise in karate meant he could protect himself and others as well. Muzila often served as a bodyguard for famous people. In fact, he had just spent four days in Las Vegas guarding TV celebrity Vanna White while she gambled at the tables. Muzila had also guarded South African bishop Desmond Tutu, TV talk show host Oprah Winfrey, karate actor Steven Seagal, and several other movie stars. The karate students had a great respect for their instructor.

After each practice, Muzila would talk for a few moments with his students and listen to their concerns. But on this particular night Muzila was the one who was concerned. "I have found out that some of you might be involved in gangs," he said to the teenage students. "This concerns me very much. Gangs are no good. They are not safe. I am not happy to learn this."

Paramount, an area south of downtown Los Angeles, is not very safe, especially at night. Many students at the local schools are involved in gangs, and there is enormous pressure on other kids to join.

Muzila warned his students that if any of them were involved in a gang, they would no longer be allowed to practice karate at his dojo. One of the students, a 13-year-old boy named Anthony, became very nervous. Anthony was in a gang, but he wanted to be in karate, too. Now he had to make a choice.

The next night Anthony left his house and walked to a nearby park, where a group of tough kids were hanging out. Anthony had an announcement to make: He was quitting the gang. His decision angered the gang leader, who told Anthony that he could not quit unless he fought five gang members at once. Anthony was frightened. But then he thought about karate. He crouched down in a karate **stance** and said, "OK, I'm ready." And the five confronted him.

Anthony showed up at the next karate practice wearing his white gi, but the uniform did not hide the bruises on his face and arms. Muzila had heard what Anthony had done and was proud of him. Fighting is never a good thing, but Muzila knew that Anthony had had to fight to free himself from the gang. Now he could remain in the karate club. Anthony continued to prac-

Muzila teaches students a controlled form of fighting called sparring.

tice three times a week, and he proudly earned a brown belt the following year.

Consider this next story. Another teenage boy in Muzila's class had always been a bully. His name was Jose, and he was taller than the other students. In karate **sparring**, opponents are not allowed to make contact by punching or kicking each other. They are supposed to pull their punches and kicks so that they stop just short of their opponent's body. This technique prevents anyone from getting hurt. But once in a while, Jose used his long arms to reach out and strike his opponent on the chin or the nose. Not too hard, but just enough so that it hurt a little. The other students were upset by Jose's behavior, but there was nothing they could do. They did not want to get into a fight with Jose.

One day during a sparring session, Jose poked another kid on the nose. Muzila saw it. "That's it, Jose," Muzila announced. "I warned you about that. Hitting someone else is not the purpose of this class. You must be punished." Muzila ordered Jose to do **squat kicks** for half an hour. A squat kick is performed by squatting down like a baseball catcher and then standing up and kicking. Doing squat kicks for half an hour is very tiring. As punishment, Jose would have to do them for 30 minutes before every class for an entire month if he wanted to remain a karate student. Muzila thought for sure that Jose would quit the dojo. To Muzila's amazement, Jose did the squat kicks before every practice for the entire month. "Jose hung in there," Muzila says. "He wouldn't quit. And by the end of the month, he had the strongest legs of any boy I'd ever seen."

Jose had changed in another way as well. He was no longer a bully. He had learned through his punishment that he had behaved badly to the other students. "The really hard work humbled him," Muzila says. "His attitude changed after that. Jose became a good karate student."

CHAPTER 2

What Karate Can Do for You

The art of karate is practiced in over 120 countries throughout the world. It is studied for a variety of reasons. To begin with, karate teaches a form of **self-defense**. In a world filled with danger that could lead to an unwanted encounter, karate provides a way out. The first thing to do if a confrontation develops is to run. Karate teaches students *not* to fight. But a person who is trapped, or is surprised from behind, will be prepared to use several methods of escape. Certain stances and **blocks** can protect a person from an attack. A variety of punches and kicks can stop the attacker and allow the karate student to get away unharmed. Initially, this is why many people practice karate.

To become skillful at such an art, students need a healthy body. It's a good idea to get a complete physical exam before you begin to do karate or any other type of exercise program. Practicing karate at least three times a week will help you become physically fit, because karate exercises the whole body. Many people, young and old, who want to develop and maintain a high level of physical fitness begin studying karate. Its movements and techniques require the use of almost all the body's muscles. Many movements in karate also require energy and stamina. It is good for the body's **respiratory system** and **circulatory system** if you take part in some form of high-energy activity at least three times a week. Karate provides this type of exercise.

"Karate teaches you a lot of things," Tom Muzila says. "It teaches you how to control your body and how to defend yourself. But even more than that, karate teaches you to have courage and to do the right thing. Karate is very mental."

What does Muzila mean by *mental*? Unlike sports that require physical ability but not much thinking, karate demands both. It is important to concentrate at all times. One of the goals of karate is to perform the kicks and punches and blocks perfectly. The student learns by repeating the movements over and over again, just as a golfer repeats the golf swing. The more times the movement is repeated correctly, the more precise it becomes. The karate student must focus on all aspects of the body—stance, balance, and the position of the arms, shoulders, head, and everything else—to achieve perfection. Students who can properly perform karate movements without looking at their hands or feet or watching themselves in the mirror have reached a point called **mind-body unity**. The body is able to do what the mind tells it to. Reaching this point takes time and a great deal of concentration or mental exercise. But it pays off in the end. Young people—male and female—who study karate generally do better in school, both with homework and on tests. Adults usually reduce their level of **stress**. All students develop a greater ability to focus and make decisions.

There is the story of a karate **master** who decided to test the focus and awareness of three of his students. He placed a small bag of sand on a ledge above the door inside his hut so that it would fall on his students as each stepped through the doorway. The master told his students to wait across the street until he gave

Self-confidence, discipline, and courage are just a few of karate's positive mental effects.

the signal. He waved to the first student to cross the street and enter his hut. As the student stepped inside, the bag of sand fell on his shoulder. The student quickly whirled around and chopped the bag into bits. "Fine," the master said. Then he motioned to the second student. This student entered the hut, and the bag of sand fell. But before it even hit him, the student stepped aside and chopped up the bag. "Very good," the master said, and then he called for the third student. This student walked across the street but stopped before entering the master's hut. The master motioned for the student to enter, but the student stood outside the doorway. The master motioned again for the student to enter, but the student pointed to the door ledge on which the bag of sand rested. "Excellent," the master said. "You have superior focus and awareness."

Karate is good for many things, but the positive mental effects that karate has on its students might be the best thing about the sport. Karate teaches self-discipline, self-control, humility, and respect for others. These are traits that everyone would like to have.

CHAPTER 3

History of Karate

The origin of karate is a mystery. **Hieroglyphics** (drawings carved into the walls of the Egyptian pyramids and dating from about 4000 B.C.) show men engaged in unarmed combat. More pictures have been found in the ruins of the ancient country of Mesopotamia (about 3000 B.C.), and there are several accounts of Greeks who used fighting techniques resembling martial arts in battles to the death.

It is widely believed that karate comes from Japan. This is a myth. The word *karate*, which is Japanese, means "empty hand." And karate as we know it today in the United States came primarily from Japan. But the first true form of karate appeared in India hundreds of years earlier. Statues and other artifacts from about 1000 B.C. show warriors in poses very much like those used in modern-day karate.

In A.D. 500, a Buddhist **monk** named Bodhidharma made a spiritual journey across India and into China. He traveled thousands of miles alone through wilderness and mountain ranges, including the majestic Himalayas. According to legend, Bodhidharma crossed the mighty Yangtze River, in central China, on a single reed. The purpose of Bodhidharma's trip was to spread knowledge. As a religious man, he did not carry any weapons, and he was therefore the victim of frequent attacks by robbers. But he was able to defeat his attackers with a form of martial art that impressed all who saw him. Eventually Bodhidharma arrived at a monastery, the home of monks. There he meditated in front of a wall for nine years and founded **Zen Buddhism**. While at the monastery, Bodhidharma also demonstrated the techniques he used for defending himself during his journey. The monks were so impressed that they adopted these skills as part of their training at the monastery. The art soon spread across China. Peasants in the country were forbidden to own weapons, and many learned the empty-handed fighting skills as a way to protect themselves.

Sometime later, karate reached the island of Okinawa, which is situated between China and Japan. Because of its location, Okinawa has historically been the victim of frequent invasions. About 500 years ago, strict laws were passed against the possession of weapons in Okinawa. The laws applied to all people living on the island, except for those in the military. The Okinawan people became worried that they would be unable to defend themselves if necessary, so they began practicing karate. All practice was done in secrecy.

During an invasion of the island in the early 1900s, the Japanese seized the weapons of the Okinawa military. But

It is wise to wear protective gear when practice involves contact.

because of their skill in karate, the Okinawan people were prepared to fight the well-trained Japanese. The invaders were so impressed that they did not fight. Instead they asked for demonstrations of this empty-handed art form. The Okinawans presented their best fighter, Gichin Funakoshi, who was only 5 feet 1 inch tall. The Japanese were skeptical, but when Funakoshi defeated several Japanese soldiers, he was invited to Japan in 1922 to demonstrate his skill. There he battled powerful sumo wrestlers and never lost. He remained in Japan for more than 30 years, teaching the art of karate, and is known today as the founder of modern karate. Funakoshi's nickname was Shoto (willow tree) because his body could bend like that tree. His style of karate, which is known as **shotokan**, is one of the largest systems of karate in the world.

Karate was introduced in Hawaii in 1927 at a YMCA in Honolulu, and Hawaiians soon began practicing the sport. The technique reached the U.S. mainland in 1946 when Robert Trias, a martial arts student, opened a karate school in Phoenix, Arizona. A student in Hawaii, Ed Parker, began teaching at Brigham Young University, in Utah, in 1954. Parker later moved to Los Angeles to teach the art to famous movie stars and performers, including actor Darren McGavin, movie producer Blake Edwards, and singer Elvis Presley, who was one of the few stars to reach the rank of black belt. In 1955, Tsutomu Ohshima arrived in Los Angeles from Japan, where he had trained under Master Funakoshi. Ohshima, a fifth-degree black belt, opened the first shotokan karate club in Los Angeles. Today there are about 130 shotokan dojos in the United States.

American soldiers and sailors stationed overseas in areas like Okinawa, Japan, and Korea were also responsible for bringing karate to the United States. These members of the service practiced karate with some of the world's greatest masters, and many of them formed karate clubs on their return to America.

Karate is still relatively new to the United States. But students of all ages and sizes are practicing karate, and its popularity is growing.

In today's violent society, many people are choosing karate, which utilizes punches and kicks, rather than dangerous forms of fighting, which require knives and guns to ward off attackers.

CHAPTER 4

A Popular Sport

One of the biggest reasons for karate's increasing popularity is its emergence, starting in the 1960s, in television and movies. Blake Edwards, the producer who learned karate from Ed Parker, put karate scenes in two of his movies—*A Shot in the Dark* and *The Pink Panther*. A television show called *The Avengers* featured actress Diana Rigg as a secret agent and master of martial arts. Robert Conrad used karate techniques to ward off foes in the TV show *The Wild Wild West*, while Bruce Lee became famous for his martial arts skills when he appeared as Kato in the television hit show *Green Hornet*. David Carradine brought more popularity to martial arts in the early 1970s with the TV program *Kung Fu*, in which a Shaolin monk named Kwai Chang Caine roams the Old West and fends off assaults from bigoted attackers. A new kung fu series returned to television in 1993, with Caine trying to teach his son that fighting is not the best way to contend with violence.

After his role as Kato, Bruce Lee became the pioneer of

martial arts movies, including *Fists of Fury*, *Enter the Dragon*, which grossed over $100 million in ticket sales, and *Return of the Dragon*. Lee died unexpectedly in 1973 from an epileptic seizure while filming *Return of the Dragon*. *Enter the Dragon* had not yet been shown in theaters, so Lee never knew how popular his last two movies would become. In *Return of the Dragon* (1973), Lee's enemy was a judo and **tang soo do** karate expert named Chuck Norris. Norris had opened a karate school in Los Angeles in 1963, and it was so successful that by 1975 he had opened six more. He gave it all up after playing the role of **nemesis** in his first film. He was such a success that producers offered him a career in movies. Norris went on to star in several of his own movies, including *Good Guys Wear Black*, *Delta Force*, *Code of Silence*, and *Octagon*. The next big star was Steven Seagal, who was a little-known martial arts instructor before arriving on the silver screen in 1988 with *Above the Law*. Seagal's second film, *Hard to Kill*, was a resounding success that made him a legitimate star. Following Seagal was Jean-Claude Van Damme, who began studying shotokan karate in Belgium when he was 11 years old. Van Damme thrust his way into the movie business by entering a Hollywood producer's office one day and performing acrobatic leaps and kicks. The producer signed him up that day for the lead role in *Bloodsport*. Van Damme has become a multimillionaire by starring in several movies since, including *Double Impact*, *Cyborg*, and *Universal Soldier*.

There are dozens of other successful martial artists who

Martial arts expert Jean-Claude Van Damme is shown here in a scene from Universal Soldier.

work behind the scenes in movies and television productions. Some appear as doubles, performing the more difficult techniques that the stars are unable to do. David Lea began practicing shotokan karate in Britain when he was 13 years old and eventually did the choreography for movies such as *Hook* and *Tango and Cash*. Lea then performed the karate scenes as a stunt double for actor Michael Keaton in *Batman*. Likewise, Kathy Long served as the stunt double for actress Michelle Pfeiffer in *Batman Returns* and has made a name for herself in Hollywood. Pat Johnson spent many years as a karate tournament referee before being discovered by the film industry. He became one of Hollywood's leading fight choreographers after making actors Pat Morita and Ralph Macchio look like karate experts in *The Karate Kid*, even though neither had ever practiced karate. Joe Corley has become a successful television producer by creating over 1,000 hours of TV programs dedicated to **full-contact karate**. Corley's shows have appeared on CBS, NBC, ESPN, and other networks, and he thinks karate contests will become a big hit on television before the year 2000.

CHAPTER 5

Karate Styles

There are over 100 different styles of karate throughout the world. While some are more popular than others, there is no style that is superior to the rest. The success of any form of karate depends on the hard work of the student and the guidance of the instructor.

Three of the most popular forms of karate in America are shotokan, tang soo do, and **tae kwon do**. Each is unique and has something positive to offer.

Shotokan, as mentioned earlier, was developed by Gichin Funakoshi in Okinawa and brought to Japan in 1922. Tsutomu Ohshima introduced the shotokan style to the United States in 1955. Shotokan features **kata**, or dancelike movements, that teach offensive and defensive techniques for a variety of situations. Shotokan emphasizes maximum power equally through swift kicks, punches, and blocks.

Tang soo do, which is the name for traditional Korean karate, originated in that country. It is similar to shotokan, but it

Tae kwon do has been chosen as the official martial art for the Olympics.

Olympic-style tae kwon do features more kicks that traditional-style tae kwon do.

has more kicks, instead of an equal amount of kicks, punches, and blocks. Sticks are used both for balance and as weapons. Tang soo do became quite popular in Korea until the 1960s, when tae kwon do was created.

Tae kwon do is a new name for Korean karate. It was created in the 1950s. There are two styles of tae kwon do: traditional and nontraditional. Traditional tae kwon do is similar to shotokan-style karate, whereas nontraditional (also known as Olympic-style tae kwon do) features mostly kicks. Tae kwon do is more dangerous than tang soo do. This martial art form is used primarily to disarm an opponent, whereas tang soo do is used more for balance. Tae kwon do has been chosen as the official martial art for the Olympics.

This martial artist is demonstrating how karate can be used to disarm a knife attacker.

CHAPTER 6

Other Martial Arts

W hile karate is certainly a popular martial art, there are a number of other types throughout the world, each deserving respect. Among the more common forms that are practiced today are **aikido, judo, ju-jitsu, kendo, kung fu,** and **tai chi**. Let's look at each.

Aikido began in Japan in the ninth century as a means to defend oneself from a weapon. Originally it featured attacks to the opponent's unprotected joints, especially the wrists and elbows. Eventually the art changed to include more body movement, wrist action, and holds. The goal is to bring the opponent's strength under control by moving with the opponent. There are said to be about 3,000 techniques in aikido. Aikidoists learn to blend or harmonize with their attacker's energy, rather than compete with it. The word *aikido* means "way of harmony," and the form is considered one of the gentler martial arts.

Judo is the most physical of all the martial arts because it requires close contact between opponents, as in wrestling. Translated, the word *ju* means "yielding" and *do* means "way of life." Unlike karate, which uses primarily punches and kicks, judo features throws. The key is to use the momentum of the opponent. As the opponent moves toward the judo student, the student grabs hold of the opponent and throws him or her forward. The object is to pull an opponent off balance with a minimum of effort and to hurl him or her to the ground.

Judo originated in Japan in the nineteenth century, and its early masters could strangle and break the limbs of several opponents at once. The sport is practiced in a much safer manner today. In fact, because it involves making contact with others and it is an Olympic sport, many young people choose to train in judo.

The art of ju-jitsu has changed considerably since it began almost 1,300 years ago in Japan. It once featured only crippling or lethal techniques. But it has since become more of a sport in which an opponent is overpowered with thrusts of the body, as in judo. One difference between the two forms is that ju-jitsu also emphasizes punches and kicks. The word *jitsu* means "fighting art."

Kendo is the Japanese art of swordsmanship. The early forms of kendo were made famous by the warriors of ancient Japan, or samurai, as they were called. Warriors were known to kill opponents brutally by cutting them in half with a sword. Kendo as practiced today is far safer because students use *shinai* (bamboo swords) and wear protective equipment. Still, the kendo student learns to deliver blows with the sword that can be lethal.

There are several other forms of armed combat such as yari-jitsu, naginata-do, and kyudo.

Kung fu is a Chinese form of martial art. The techniques of kung fu have been patterned after movements in animals. One form, which is based on the tiger, features a firm stance, powerful attacks, and the tiger-claw formation of the hand. Another form is similar to the monkey—it uses crouching defensive positions, escaping rolls, and attacking leaps. Other forms are similar to the praying mantis and the crane. Kung fu is more than 4,000 years old, and it continues to grow in popularity.

Tai chi is also known as *tai chi chuan*, which translates as "supreme ultimate fist." But tai chi today has little to do with the fist. Instead it is an extremely gentle martial art that is performed almost in slow motion. The goal is to bring the body into harmony through a series of 108 movements. While tai chi can be used to ward off an attacker, it is performed mainly for health, relaxation, and mental balance.

Karate students are taught to master basic moves like the front kick.

CHAPTER 7

Mastery of the Art

There are three basic parts to the study of karate. First is **kihon**, or basic blocks, punches, and kicks. Second is kata, or dancelike movements. Third is **kumite**, or sparring. Mastery of the art cannot be achieved unless all three parts are studied with equal attention. To be consistent in our description of the art of karate, we will use a specific style—shotokan—as the model.

In order to learn the basics, the karate student must first have the proper balance. There are seven stances in shotokan karate. The most common is the front stance, in which the front foot is placed forward, with knee bent; the distance between the feet is about 1 yard. Weight is evenly distributed between feet, with both heels on the floor. The back stance is the opposite of the front stance, and most of the weight is on the back foot. The horse stance resembles sitting on a horse, as the feet are wider apart and the toes are turned slightly outward. Other stances are the cat stance, feet-together stance, natural stance, and immovable stance.

These students are practicing the crescent moon kick stance.

There are also seven **hand attacks**–the regular fist, spear hand, sword hand, elbow, knuckle point, back fist, and ridge-hand.

It is widely accepted that karate has the most developed **foot techniques** of any martial art. The featured kicks, among a wide variety, are the front kick, side kick, back kick, hook kick, knee kick, roundhouse kick, crescent moon kick, and stamp-in kick. Each is practiced by beginners and experts alike. Other kicks include the jump kick, double kick, and side thrust kick.

Keeping both eyes on the opponent is necessary in karate.

A good arm block is used to ward off an attacker.

Blocks are considered one of the most important aspects of karate. In sparring, a good block can make the opponent lose balance. The student performs the technique primarily by allowing the opponent to deliver the first blow and then blocking it. The student can then counter the attack. Some key blocks include the scooping block, hooking block, sweeping block, down block, and hammer block. There are several others to learn as well.

To execute the techniques effectively, the student should be flexible. A good karate class will always include at least ten minutes of warm-up exercises to stretch the body before practicing the basics.

Next is kata. To the observer, kata appears to be a dance in which the student is kicking, blocking, and punching an imaginary opponent. This is partly true. What the observer cannot see,

A punching bag is used for side kick practice.

The side thrust kick requires good balance and control.

however, is the mind of the student. With practice, the student should develop a calmness or peace of mind while performing kata.

Kata is a series of movements that lasts about one minute. They are performed at a certain tempo—either slow, fast, or from fast to slow, or from slow to fast—depending on the kata. There are 19 different kata in shotokan, each unique in its own way. One aspect of all kata is that the student begins and ends from the same spot on the floor. The first kata learned by all shotokan karate students is **taikyoku shodan**. It is a series of downward blocks and front punches—two of the most basic movements in karate.

In some karate styles there are a wide variety of belt colors. They are, from beginner to expert: white, yellow, orange, green, brown, and black. There are ten levels (degrees) of black belt. In shotokan karate, however, there are only three colors: white, brown, and black. To attain a higher rank, the student must demonstrate proficiency in the techniques required for the next rank. Demonstrations are done in front of a licensed examiner or group of examiners. It is said that to fully understand a kata, the student must perform that kata at least 10,000 times. This requires several years of practice.

The word *kumite* is Japanese for sparring. The technique allows students to practice their offensive and defensive skills against one another in supervised combat. Karate sparring is relatively safe. When delivering a punch or a kick to an opponent, the student aims to *miss*. An expert will come within a fraction of an

This student is working to perfect his kicking.

inch of striking the opponent. Still, the blow will not connect. The purpose of kumite is to practice the techniques without hurting anybody and to prepare oneself in case the techniques might be needed.

Several forms of kumite are practiced. The most basic is ippon-kumite (one-step sparring). In ippon-kumite, the student attacks once with either a midlevel or a face-level punch. The opponent first defends himself or herself with any number of blocks, then counters with a punch or kick. Another form is sambon-kumite (three-step sparring). In this, the student attacks with

Dojo members work together to learn all they can about the art of karate.

three midlevel or face-level punches, and the opponent again defends himself or herself with blocks, then counters with a blow. Finally, there is jiyu-kumite (free sparring), in which the two opponents are allowed to attack and defend as they wish.

There are other forms of kumite, but ippon-kumite, sambon-kumite, and jiyu-kumite are the most common. Again, it must be understood by all who practice karate that attacks are to be stopped short of connecting.

Before engaging in kumite (or entering the dojo), students customarily bow (**rei**) as a show of respect to the opponent (or dojo).

To be competent at karate, the student must learn several things. The first is breath control and **kiai** (a loud shout). For the student to achieve speed in attacks, the body must be relaxed. It is important to breathe slowly while practicing. Breathing may seem natural, but it is easily forgotten when the student is thinking about other things, like blocking an attack. A kiai is made when delivering a kick or a punch, and it is necessary for two reasons: It creates extra force from the body, and it can momentarily frighten the opponent. There is an old story of a karate master who was meditating in the mountains when he was attacked by a tiger. As the tiger charged, the master kiaied so loudly that the tiger turned and ran away.

The second important elements in karate are focus and timing. The expert is able to focus all his or her concentration and energy on a pinpoint target. This is what gives karate masters the power to smash through wood or bricks. Timing is important especially during kumite. The karate expert needs only a split-second of time to block an opponent's attack and counter with an attack.

Spirit and attitude are the third components in determining a skillful karate student. It is important to be enthusiastic at all times, whether practicing basics against an imaginary opponent or sparring against a real opponent. The best karate students have the strongest spirit.

The fourth, and final, element is to understand that the purpose of karate is not to beat up people. Students who don't

Muzila teaches his students the importance of balance while performing the straight punch.

understand the purpose are failing at karate. In the movie *Teenage Mutant Ninja Turtles*, one of the turtles, Raphael, is behaving so aggressively that his master, Splinter, must warn him. The first rule of martial arts, Splinter tells Raphael, "is to possess the right thinking. Only then can one receive the gifts of strength, knowledge, and peace. I have tried to channel your anger, Raphael, but more remains. Anger clouds the mind. Turned inward, it is an unconquerable enemy." Raphael must learn to be peaceful to others, even to those who are not always nice to him. This is a true test of courage and inner strength.

CHAPTER 8

The Real Opponent

When fifth-degree black belt Tom Muzila decided to practice karate as a 15-year-old boy, he searched everywhere for a good dojo. At the time, Muzila was hanging out with tough kids and was interested mostly in fighting. One night he spotted a dojo in Long Beach, California, and he went inside. "I couldn't believe the fighting," Muzila says. "People were being thrown all over the place. There were big guys and small guys, and all of them were tough. It was like a battlefield." He joined the dojo that night.

Two significant changes have occurred since those days 30 years ago. First, we no longer find students "being thrown all over the place." The sport is much more controlled now. If karate students tried to beat each other up, soon there would be no one left in the dojo to practice. Second, Muzila's interest in karate changed. He began to appreciate the sport for what it really is—a martial art that gives students better understanding and control of themselves. This is what karate instructors are supposed to teach their students.

In the movie *The Karate Kid*, Daniel is being picked on by several bullies from his school. Daniel's instructor, Mr. Miyagi, teaches him the purpose of karate in this exchange:

"Fighting is always last answer to problem," Mr. Miyagi says.

"No offense, Mr. Miyagi, but I don't think you understand my problem," Daniel says.

"Problem is attitude," Mr. Miyagi tells him. "Boys have bad attitude. Karate for self-defense only."

"That's not what these guys are taught," Daniel says.

"I can see," says Mr. Miyagi. "No such thing as bad student. Only bad teacher. Teacher say, student do."

With karate, or any form of martial art, it is important to find a good instructor, one who emphasizes that fighting is *not* the purpose of the sport.

Lisa Bluemel is a black-belt instructor who teaches shotokan karate in San Diego. Bluemel says that it is also important to find a class that has many types of students—black belts and white belts, men and women, children and older people. "When I was young, I thought that you had to be a big, tough guy to be in karate," she says. "But I learned that it is just as good for young boys and for women and girls as it is for men." About 30 students practice regularly in Bluemel's dojo in San Diego, and more than half are women.

By watching an expert demonstration, members of this karate class are striving to learn from the pros and possibly become future black belts themselves.

Tom Muzila says that karate is especially good for kids and teens. "Learning karate gives them self-confidence and teaches them to express themselves and open up in new ways. It teaches them to focus, which helps them with their schoolwork. Most of the kids in my class are getting much better grades since they started training," he says.

There are numerous benefits to practicing karate. Self-confidence. Courage. Discipline and self-control. Improved focus, which could mean better grades. And a great way to exercise. So don't be afraid to start. The only real opponent, you will soon discover, is yourself.

To Find Out More About Karate

BOOKS

Barrett, Norman. *Martial Arts*. (Picture Library). 1989. Franklin Watts.

Brimner, Larry Dane. *Karate*. 1988. Franklin Watts.

Jennings, Joseph. *Winning Karate*. 1982. Contemporary Books.

Kauz, Herman. *The Martial Spirit*. 1991. Overlook Press.

Lewis, Tom G. *Karate for Kids*. 1980. National Paperback Book Publishers.

Neff, Fred. *Lessons from the Samurai: Ancient Self-Defense Strategies and Techniques*. 1987. Lerner Publications.

Nishiyama, Hidetaka, and Brown, Richard C. *Karate: Art of Empty-Hand Fighting*. 1991. Charles E. Tuttle Company.

Parulski, George R. *Karate's Modern Masters*. 1985. Contemporary Books.

WHERE TO WRITE FOR INFORMATION

Black Belt Magazine
24715 Avenue Rockefeller, P.O. Box 918
Santa Clarita, CA 91380

President's Council on Physical Fitness and Sports
Suite 250, 701 Pennsylvania Avenue NW
Washington, DC 20004

Shotokan Karate of America
2500 South La Cienega Boulevard
Los Angeles, CA 90034

Glossary

aikido A gentle form of martial art. Aikidoists learn to redirect or harmonize with their opponent's energy without harm to either person.

block A method of preventing an opponent's attack, primarily by warding off the blow with one's arms or feet.

circulatory system The system by which blood is transported throughout the body.

dojo The building in which students practice karate.

foot techniques Specific movements, such as kicking, that require use of the foot only.

full-contact karate A martial art form in which opponents intentionally try to strike one another.

gi The uniform (usually white) that karate students wear.

hand attack A form of delivering a blow to an opponent by using various hand techniques.

hieroglyphics Ancient drawings often found on sculptures and cave walls.

judo A martial art similar to wrestling that features throws.

ju-jitsu A martial art that combines throws with punches and kicks.

kata Kicks and punches practiced in specific dancelike movements.

kendo A martial art featuring swords.

kiai A loud shout given when delivering a kick or punch.

kihon The basic blocks, punches, and kicks used in karate.

kumite The Japanese word for sparring, a controlled form of fighting between two opponents.

kung fu A martial art similar to boxing and patterned after the movements of animals.

master A high-ranking expert who teaches and guides the karate student.

mind-body unity A stage in which the body does what the mind tells it to do.

monk A person who lives quietly under strict religious rules.

nemesis A person who seeks vengeance.

rei To bow (bend forward at the waist) as a show of respect.

respiratory system The system that provides the body with oxygen and rids it of carbon dioxide.

self-defense The act of protecting oneself from harm.

shotokan The most common style of karate in the world. Shotokan emphasizes swift kicks, punches, and blocks.

sparring A controlled form of fighting between two opponents.

squat kick A technique performed by crouching down, then standing up and kicking.

stance Method of standing to assure balance.

stress The feeling of anxiety or nervousness, often caused by problems in one's life.

tae kwon do A martial art featuring kicks. Tae kwon do is primarily used to disable a person.

tai chi A gentle martial art usually performed very slowly.

taikyoku shodan A series of downward blocks and front punches. It is the first kata learned by shotokan karate students.

tang soo do A martial art that emphasizes balance and features an equal amount of kicks and punches.

Zen Buddhism A religion of enlightenment introduced into China in the sixth century and into Japan in the twelfth century.

Index